in a HURRY

Middle Ages

written and drawn by
JOHN FARMAN

MACMILLAN
CHILDREN'S BOOKS

First published 1998 by Macmillan Children's Books
a division of Macmillan Publishers Limited
25 Eccleston Place, London SW1W 9NF
and Basingstoke

Associated companies throughout the world

ISBN 0 330 35252 0

Text and illustrations copyright © John Farman 1998

The right of John Farman to be identified as the
author of this work has been asserted by him in accordance with the
Copyright, Designs and Patents Act 1988.

1 3 5 7 9 8 6 4 2

A CIP catalogue record for this book is available from
the British Library.

Printed and bound in Great Britain
by Mackays of Chatham plc, Kent

CONTENTS

Off we go!   **4**

1 Some Historical Comings and Goings   **5**

2 Naughty but Nice: Outlaws   **20**

3 Mid-Knights   **25**

4 Serfing in the Middle Ages   **30**

5 Who Owned What: The Toffs Battle it Out   **36**

6 Middle-Aged Food   **38**

7 Feeling Poorly in the Middle Ages   **41**

8 Middle-Aged Children   **49**

9 Town Life   **52**

10 Witch Report   **55**

11 Art, Science, God and all that   **61**

Time's Up   **64**

༄ OFF WE GO!

There seems to be a bit of an argument about when the Middle Ages started and finished. Proper historians (loads of GCSEs and stuff) include the whole bit from the Romans leaving Britain in AD 410, right up to the middle of the fifteenth century, including the Dark Ages. The Dark Ages, you see, were at the beginning of the Middle Ages – but as there are only 64 pages in this book, I've split 'em into two: so the Dark Ages go from AD 410 to 1066 and *my* Middle Ages start from when William the well-known Conqueror turned the English into Normans (in 1066). If you understand all that you deserve 10/10 for comprehension.*

PS You might see bossy little comments (like the one below) throughout the book. They're written by my editor, Susie; she seems to have a very low boredom threshold.

Middle-Aged Kings and Coronations			
William I	1066	Edward III	1327
William II	1087	Richard II	1377
Henry I	1100	Henry IV	1399
Stephen	1135	Henry V	1413
Henry II	1154	Henry VI	1422
Richard I	1189	Edward IV	1461
John	1199	Edward V	1483
Henry III	1216	Richard III	1483
Edward I	1272	Henry VII	1485
Edward II	1307	Henry VIII	1509

*Just get on with it. Ed

Chapter 1

SOME HISTORICAL COMINGS AND GOINGS

Harold and Co.

As you might know, well before 1066 most of the English Vikings that had set up home in Britain had run off to be Norman Vikings in Normandy, which had kindly been given to them (under just a little pressure) by the French king Charles the Bald around AD 900. Over the years, and after marrying loads of French girls, several at a time (as most Vikings did), they gradually became just plain, ordinary Normans (as most Normans are) – but still a powerful force to reckon with. So much so that by 1066, having been squinting at us menacingly across the channel, they took the plunge, popped across and conquered us. Harold, our current king, was luckily *not* killed by catching an arrow in the eye (as history usually informs us) but unluckily died in the battle all the same (probably tripping over the guy who *was*).

Norman – sorry – William the Conqueror

William had an easy job conquering England – especially London. We apparently offered little resistance (which might have been because our armies were always in the wrong place at the wrong time). William promptly made himself king (who wouldn't?) and got down to the rather awkward job of taking all the land off all the English noblemen who were still alive and divvying it up amongst his own lads as a present for all their hard work (a kind of loyalty bonus). He then adopted the dead clever 'feudalism' system, which went something like this:

1. Most people from then on were to be tenants; that is, would pay rent. The King, you see, had made sure he owned everything and everyone. Smart move.

2. Tenants-in-chief (all Normans) were given vast estates to play with . . . provided they rustled up enough knights and soldiers every now and again to fight for the king and sometimes go Crusading (persuading heathens to be Christian – and killing 'em if they argued). Even smarter move.

3. Below him were freemen, who farmed anything up to thirty acres and paid a rent to their overlord. Quite smart for those concerned.

4. At the very bottom was the 'serf' or 'villain'* who had a piece of land the size of your average backyard (if he was lucky) which he was able to grow stuff on provided he paid rent and worked a proportion of his time on his master's vast acres. The common serf and his common wife were able to share the common land with his common neighbours. He was not a freeman and could not leave the area without permission. Smart if you were William or the overlord in question, but not very smart if you were the serf.

Keeping Track
The tenants-in-chief were like little dictators, running their huge estates as they pleased. They even administered the law and, as there was no parliament, advised William about how their bit of the country was ticking over. Just to make sure they,

*Shouldn't that be 'villein'? Ed

or anyone else, didn't try to con him, in 1085 William ordered a humungous volume called the Domesday Book. In this work (completed in 1086), with the help of millions of minions, he listed everything he owned throughout the land, right down to the last hovel and the last teaspoon.*

Useless and Extremely Unpleasant Fact No. 453

William, who was the son of Robert the Magnificent (great surname), was known as a great fighter and was to be seen on horseback at all major battles. Unfortunately, he had become so fat by the time he fought the French at Mantes he could hardly get into the saddle. He died when his horse reared, stumbling on a burning timber. Witnesses say he shot into the air and landed right on the metal bit of the saddle (ouch!), which caught him fair and square between the legs and burst his bowels (and no doubt made his eyes water).

In 1087 William's boy William Rufus succeeded him, and in 1100 William Rufus's brother succeeded him and became Henry I. By the time Henry died at 11.35**, nobody with any sense could really argue that the Norman Conquest had been anything but a jolly good thing. The English had stopped fighting each other and became rather tame and almost docile. Not only that but, because we were now run by foreigners, we had a much closer rapport with abroad (instead of being conquered by them every five minutes).

Mayhem

All good things come to an end (just look at my hair), and as

*Tea didn't come to England until the seventeenth century. Ed
**Shouldn't that be 'in 1135'? Ed

soon as Henry was gone, all the barons (tenants-in-chief, etc.) started fighting each other . . . for twenty years! They all wanted to climb onto the throne or slither under that big shiny hat. To try to describe the next bit in the fine, detailed and uncannily perceptive manner that I'm famous for* would take far longer than I've got, so just take it from me that all the kings in the next bit seemed to be called Henry (apart from John and Richard) and all their wives and daughters Matilda (apart from the few that weren't).

Henry Holds Out

In 1154, Henry II put a stop to all the fighting and squabbling for the throne between his grandad Henry I's daughter Matilda (from Henry I's marriage to a Matilda) and Stephen (grandson of William the Conqueror – also married to a Matilda) who married – three guesses – a Matilda. Confused yet? Me too.

He became king of all England (and a fair chunk of France into the bargain) by marrying the *très* stroppy Mademoiselle Eleanor of Aquitaine. To make everything nice and peaceful again, he let the English people keep a check on the feudal nobility (barons, earls, etc.) rather than the other way round, as his great-grandad William had done. Then he dumped all the sheriffs and their tin-pot local courts and set up proper courts with proper juries and proper judges who wore proper judge's outfits. All those terrible but rather fab trials by torture went out of the courtroom window.

Useless and Rather Dubious Fact No. 457

Henry had a long-standing mistress called Fair Rosamund of Woodstock. It was said that to keep his wife away from her he built an amazing maze in front of her house. It was also said that

*Just who are you kidding? Ed

Eleanor turned out to be rather good at mazes and managed to get to Fair Rosamund and murder her anyway. The fact that Eleanor was actually in prison at the time doesn't seem to have hindered her (or history come to that). You can't keep a good story down.

YOU COULD TRY ROUND THE BACK

Gay Richard (1189–99)

I think it quite brill that King Richard the Lionheart, Henry's son and perhaps the greatest macho hero we've ever had (after Mrs Thatcher of course), was almost certainly homosexual. During his reign he was away quite a bit in France or cruising – sorry – *crusading* in Asia, trying to teach the Muslims and their boss Saladin a lesson for not being Christians. In fact he only spent six months in England during his whole ten-year reign.

Useless Fact No. 460

Richard married the dead gorgeous Berengaria of Navarre but despite her astounding beauty they had no kids. He didn't have any illegitimate ones either – almost unheard of in those days. Why could this be? Suggestions on a postcard, please.

'Orrible John

While Richard was away playing heroes, his brother – the extremely unpleasant John* – got up to all sorts of mischief,

*Are all Johns extremely unpleasant? *Ed*
I hope you're not referring to me. *JF*

robbing the poor to pay the rich while living in luxury and trying to kill our dear old Robin Hood, who robbed the rich to pay the poor while living in . . . trees. Actually catching old Robin must have proved a trifle tricky, seeing as history now reckons he didn't really exist.

Magna Carta

Anyway, apart from being very nasty and a very bad king, John is best remembered for being forced into signing a huge document, the Magna Carta, in 1215, which gave away a lot of royal power to the barons and helped create loads of firemen.*
After the signing he returned to Windsor Castle where his behaviour was said to be 'that of a frantic madman for, besides swearing, he gnashed his teeth, rolled his eyes and gnawed sticks and straw' – how odd! In the end, the English invited Louis of France to whiz over and have a go on the English throne (quelle cheek!), but he seemed not to like the idea and went home pretty smartish. John died in the same year (1216) on the evening of October 18, when he suddenly keeled over, having eaten a hearty meal – followed by peaches and cider. Some say he was poisoned, but I think he simply ate himself to death.

*I think you mean 'freemen'. Ed

Little Henry

John's boy Henry III took over aged nine. He meant well, ran a fabulous court and had oodles of smart friends and all that sort of thing, but got Britain into even more trub than they'd been in before. Henry hacked everyone off: he seemed almost to be on a mission to undo any good work that had gone before. He got his foreign friends into all the best positions of power, and worse than that, started becoming uncomfortably pally with the Roman Catholics, especially the Pope.

Edward I

In 1272 his son Edward took over. He was dead popular with his subjects because he managed to reduce the powers of the barons and parliament *and* the Church. The downside of all this was a nasty nationalism (thinking that your country's best) amongst the masses, which resulted in all the Jews and other miscellaneous 'foreigners' being kicked out. Then, just for good measure, he rammed down the lid on the stroppy Welsh who'd been getting a bit above themselves, and left a load of fully-armed castles to keep them in their place.

But why stop now, he thought to himself? Let's do Scotland next.

Stealing Scones

So saying, he promptly crossed the border and gave the Scots a really bad time, stealing their Stone of Scone – a chunk of old rock on which, for no reason that I know of, they'd always crowned their kings. The Scots, seriously narked, responded by making a fierce chieftain, Robert the Bruce (what's a Bruce?), their king. He immediately looked round for allies to help teach the British a lesson. And who did he come up with? Now think; who, apart from the Irish, the Welsh, the Indians, the Spanish, the Germans (and two-thirds of the civilized world) have traditionally hated the English? The French – *naturellement*. Unfortunately, poor Eddie died in 1307 on the way to the first proper battle with the newly formed McFrench, so it was left to his son to Carry On Fighting.

Useless Fact No. 462

Edward had been quite a cool customer. Once, after the Battle of Lewes, when he was held prisoner (with his dad, brother and horse) by Simon de Montfort, he challenged his captors to a horse race. Little did they know that his steed was famous for its speed, and the twerps watched him literally gallop off into the sunset. (Nice one, Eddie!)

More Edwards

Edward I's son, Edward II, was worse than his dad at getting on with the neighbours, and made the situation with Scotland, Wales *and* France appalling rather than just awful. He was an odd chap by all accounts – but quite a laugh, being most talked about for his 'more than close' relationship with a camp follower or court hanger-on called Piers Gaveston – but we won't go into that now.*

In the meantime, Robert the Bruce of Scotland, fed up with being pushed around, decided to go on the offensive and started ram-raiding the north of England, before snatching Ireland. By this time the English barons had had enough of

*You surprise me. Ed

Edward II, especially the way he kept giving his friend Piers everything he wanted, including leaving him in charge when he went off to get himself the almost obligatory French wife (who was aged 12). Thus started a sort of crazy tennis match, with the advantage swapping on every serve.

Edward v The Barons – The Match

👑 First the barons grabbed Parliament and chopped off Gaveston's head . . . *15–LOVE*.

👑 They, in turn, were as bad at running England as Edward had been, so the country got behind old Eddie again and allowed him, after a couple of fierce battles, to take all his power back . . . *15–ALL*.

👑 But then, just as he thought he'd sorted it, his dear wife and her lover (she'd obviously become a little bored with being married to a homosexual), backed by a bunch of beastly barons, captured him . . . *30–15*

👑 . . . and made him give up being king . . . *40–15*.

👑 He ended his days imprisoned in a disused well* at Berkeley Castle in Gloucestershire and was murdered in 1327 . . . *GAME, SET AND MATCH*.

Useless and Disturbing Fact No. 465

Isabella, Edward's wife, really couldn't have liked her hubby that much. On her instructions, he was killed by having a horn rammed up his bottom and a red-hot poker inserted into said horn (see Great Ways of Getting Rid of a King by Creating Maximum Pain and Leaving Minimum Visible Evidence).

And Another Edward

Next up was Edward (son of Edward)'s son Edward (good at names, weren't they?). This one was the IIIrd and was a bit of

* Doesn't that make it a used well? Ed
All right, a well-used well. JF

a 'bloke' by all accounts – lots of enthusiasm but behind the door when brains were given out. He loved spending money, especially on himself, but best of all drinking, dancing, sport and fighting (sounds like dear old Gazza) – with anyone and everyone. It was this love of fighting, added to an inherited lack of diplomacy, that got England into the Hundred Years' War (1338–1453)* with France, a war that was to bring England to its knees cash-wise. All those swords, soldiers and horses (*and* the ships to get them to the punch-up) cost a fortune, you know – certainly more than England or Edward (who poured a lot of his own cash into the war-pot) could afford.

Useless Fact No. 467

Edward III eventually went personally bankrupt – the first and last monarch to do so. (I wonder if that could ever happen to our lot . . .?)

The Black Prince

Edward's favourite fighting mate was his son (Edward) the Black Prince (so called because of his fab black armour). Between them they fought the French at the Battle of Crécy and managed to kill 15,000 of the poor Frogs while losing only 400 of their own personal soldiers. In fact all was going swimmingly well until something happened that was to stop both sides in their tracks. What could it be? Any ideas?

Clue: What makes you go black and kills you?

Plague Alert

Imagine coming home one evening and seeing on the Six O'Clock News that a disease called the Black Death was about to hit England *and* was more easily caught than any other disease in history *and* that once caught couldn't be recovered

*That's more than a hundred years. Ed

from *and* ended in a horribly painful death. *That* might put you off your fish fingers.

It appears that a bunch of filthy eastern fleas had hitched a lift on a bunch of filthy eastern rats, who'd hitched a lift on an eastern boat (presumably filthy too) to Europe. Equally filthy old England was a marvellous breeding ground for the virus, and by the time the plague had run out of steam it had accounted for well over a third – yes, a third – of the population of Britain, which meant that there simply wasn't anyone around to fight France *with*. Luckily, for us, they'd had *Le Plague* too (though not nearly as badly) and were in the same boat.

Useless Fact No. 469
The Black Death was so powerful that even dogs and cats (and budgies?*) died from it. However, the frightened folk killed all their pets anyway as they thought they carried the virus.

War Money
Luckily for them, both Eddie and his son survived the plague, but by 1377 the old man had gone round the bend anyway and the Black Prince was dead from fighting just once too often. But the Black Prince's little ten-year-old lad, Richard II (the result of his dad's liaison with a lady called, rather weirdly, the Fair Maid of Kent), rather liked the idea of slaughtering Frenchmen (in those days you didn't need much of a reason for a good war) and charged every English peasant 5p (about £20

*They didn't have budgies. Ed

today) to pay for his sport. Quite reasonable, eh? Well, reasonable enough, until you consider that the poor so-and-serfs only earned ½p (£2) a day.

Then, in 1396, Richard spoilt it all by marrying a right royal French dame called Isabelle de Valois who was dead cute, but unfortunately only seven (don't ask) and that seemed to stop the war with France in its tracks. Love, it appears – or rather, an arranged marriage to a child – conquered all in those days. As a matter of interest, by the time the Hundred Years' 'Expensive' War was over, France had got all its land back apart from Calais, which for some reason we seemed to have got rather attached to (probably all that cheap booze and smelly cheese).

Useless Fact No. 471

Nobody knows how Richard died, but in Clifford Brewer's brilliant book *A Medical History of the Kings and Queens of England*, he suggests that he was poisoned by a Death Cap toadstool chopped up in his supper. They did love their poisoning, bless 'em.

Useless Fact No. 473

One of the worst jobs in medieval times was to be the king's Official Food-Taster. He had to try everything the king ate, just in case someone had dropped something in it. Well-paid, admittedly, but with pretty poor long-term prospects. It really was a case of 'heads you lose, tails you lose'. What's the point of doing a job really well if the end result is a death-most-horrid through poisoning?

Here Comes Henry Again

True to form, however, Richard was murdered by Henry soon-to-be IV, the Black Prince's nephew, who'd been exiled in France. He came back to grab his inheritance, which was all

the lands and property of the recently dead John of Gaunt (the Black Prince's brother and his dad)* – which he did. The first part of his reign was a nightmare, with poor Henry wearing down his horse's legs dashing the length and breadth of his lands, trying to keep his enemies at bay. Eventually, he got it straight and the last eight or nine years were rather peaceful but, for our purposes, rather boring.

I THINK YOU MIGHT NEED A NEW 'ORSE YOUR MAJESTY

Useless Fact No. 475

Henry was a fine young man of good health but suffered from a plague of lice throughout his life and was never able to grow hair properly. (I know the feeling).

The Last Bit

Henry V (Hal to his friends) had been a right nutter when young – drinking, fighting, gambling and mixing with a bunch of sad old drunks, but when he got the top job of King he really shaped up and became rather serious (bit of a shame). His only remaining vice was persecuting anyone that didn't agree with

* How could he have been the Black Prince's brother *and* father? Ed
Read it again, silly. John of Gaunt was his dad. JF.

him God-wise (especially a bunch of Christian rebels, nicknamed Lollards). His only *other* remaining vice was to continue to harass the French. Mind you, they'd been doing it to us for centuries, so yah-boo, I say.

It all came to a head at the battle of Agincourt which we won hands down, basically because our longbows were quicker to reload than their crossbows. Then, just to console the French, who believed they were going to lose everything, he married the daughter of their king, Charles the Silly (who was as mad as a gateau) and ended up being Regent (nearly king) of (nearly all) France.

The Even Laster Bit
In 1422 Henry Vth had a little VIth called . . . you're right . . . Henry. The wee chappie became a kinglet after only nine months of princedom, daddy having died of something (or someone) he'd picked up in France. He had a relatively easy time as a child, apart from being niggled by a French transvestite (she wore men's armour) called Joan, who'd been living on a sort of houseboat.* Joan of Arc led a French rebellion against the English (because some dead saints had told her to) but ended up being roasted in 1431 in Rouen and having her ashes thrown into the river . . . presumably to put them out.

Roses are Forever
Henry VI was mad. Luckily, his missus, Margaret, wasn't and therefore acted for him when times got tough. The Great Civil War in England was all about roses. Apparently, she liked red ones, but the Duke of York and the Earl of Warwick were rather partial to white. Actually, I believe there was a little

*I think you'll find that Arc doesn't mean the same as ark. *Ed*

more to it than that, but I don't have time to go into it now.

The Wars of the Roses went on for years. First of all the Yorkists beat Margaret and the Lancastrians (weren't they in the charts a couple of years ago?) good and proper. Poor old Henry ended up in the Bloody Tower where he was eventually murdered to death and Margaret (the wife) quietly crept over to France where she opened a bed and breakfast* and died in poverty. On the other side, Warwick fell off his horse and couldn't move (heavy armour involved) which made him a sitting duke (a dead one). Edward IV, son of Richard, Duke of York, became the new king but, after reigning for twenty years, died from too much of everything.

My Kingdom For a Horse
After yet another Edward (the fifth), the famous Richard III appeared, who was hated by all and sundry. He lost the final battle between the Yorks and the Lancastrians (and was killed rather badly while trying to negotiate a rather one-sided deal on a horse). You remember – the 'my kingdom for a horse' speech.

Henry VII practically caught the crown before it hit the ground in 1485, and married Elizabeth of the Yorks which brought the two families much closer together (especially the bride and groom). This heralded the end of the Wars of the Roses and effectively (mostly because I've run out of words for this chapter) the end of my historical rundown.

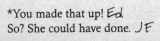

*You made that up! Ed
So? She could have done. JF

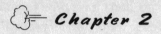

Chapter 2

NAUGHTY BUT NICE: OUTLAWS

Just like the Great Train Robbers, outlaws and vagabonds in the Middle Ages often became folk-heroes, because many of them got kicks from making fools of the rich. And once a legend was established, their dastardly doings were embellished – often to fairy-tale proportions. So, although Robin Hood is better known for his telly series (and pantos) and Hereward the Wake and William Tell look more at home on a Hollywood film set, they do give a clue as to what the real bandits were actually like. It must be said that in those days, most people turned to crime not because they were inherently naughty, but because circumstances forced them into it (like all their money and land being stolen by the local barons or the church).

Forgiveness for Sale

One of the chief targets to any would-be R. Hoods or W. Tells were the corrupt and seriously rich monks, abbots, and friars (unlike Tuck, of course) who travelled the land like royalty, living off the poor and selling indulgences (see chapter 7). Outlaws, you see, were mostly portrayed as being very loyal to the king, and being rather concerned with exposing all the corruption that went on just below him. Here are a few of the best outlaws of the Middle Ages . . .

Lionel, King of the Rout of Raveners (gang of plunderers)

You're right, these days anyone with a name like Lionel sounds like they either work in a bank or a hairdresser's, but this Lionel was a fearful brigand from the mid-fourteenth century. He was dead cool, wearing a home-made crown and employing his own bunch of bloodthirsty lieutenants to do his bidding. He was passionately loyal to King Edward the IIIrd and to God the Ist and spent much of his time righting the wrongs that he considered had been done in the king's name – in a somewhat violent manner.

The Beckwiths of Beckwithshaw

A bunch of outlaws called Beckwith? I don't think so. But yes, at around the same time as old Lionel was a-plundering, this happy family led a spectacular revolt on behalf of the northern counties against John of Gaunt, who they accused of taking all their rights (which he had). These guys really were proper fully paid-up outlaws, living literally 'outside the law'. The cheeky things set up their own parliament and abided by their own set of rules which, as you might guess, didn't have a lot to do with the laws of the land. Therefore, if whatever they did seemed to go with their version of 'OK', they went and did it. Neat, but don't try this at home (or at school).

Sir William Stapleton

William Stapleton of Cumberland had none of those high-fallutin' loyalties to king, country or God. His was simply a dreadful dispute with his wicked stepmum Mary, who snatched all of his father's (her husband's) estates and manor houses (and therefore little Willie's inheritance and future) when the old chap croaked. Stapleton Jnr did some rather persuasive things to bring her to reason, like torching the family's woodlands, capturing whole manor houses and holding up government officials carrying important documents. When he was finally outlawed in 1444 he took to the hills and was never seen again. Which just goes to show.*

William Wallace

Famous Scot William Wallace was more of a rebel than an outlaw, and for years was known as *Sir* William Wallace, though nobody seems to know when he was knighted or who did him (so to speak). I think he must've made it up. He lived in the second half of the thirteenth century and was famous for putting a spanner into the attempts of Edward I to take over bonnie Scotland. He was captured in 1305 and hanged, drawn and quartered in London. He then travelled to Newcastle, Berwick, Sterling and Perth – unfortunately, as you might imagine, all at the same time. That's quartering for you! Robert the famous Bruce, having played dead for over a year on Rathlin Island, took over where he left off, and continued to fight the English.

*What? Ed

Hereward the Wake (the watchful one)

One of those that got the royal pardon was Hereward the Wake who led a rebellion against William in 1070. He operated out of the Isle of Ely (which isn't an island any more, cos someone took the plug out of the fens and drained them to make Cambridgeshire).

Bonded

When William conquered England in 1066, thousands of men who had once been freemen became bonded to their overlords, which was a bit of a poor show. These 'bondmen' could only escape by breaking the law and becoming, as the word 'vagabonds' suggests, vagrant. Vagabonds would tour the kingdom begging, robbing churches (chalices and candlesticks and stuff) and even graves (bones and stuff?). Some even came over from France for the rich pickings (why couldn't they rob their own churches, eh?)

ISN'T THIS YOUR UNCLE HARRY?

In 1196 a law was made stating that you could never put up strangers or even friends for more than two nights (sounds fine to me) in an effort to prevent the harbouring of said vagabonds. If you were a freeman, you risked serfdom if you sheltered such a person, so the only alternative for the poor devils was to join the many gangs of outlaws. King William was rather sporting about the whole business, decreeing that if you could avoid arrest for more than two years you qualified for a royal pardon and would remain free for ever. I bet some modern-day criminals wished that little decree still stood!

Useless Fact No. 479

Throughout Europe it became common for down-and-outs to have to obtain a 'licence to beg'. Sporting a little beggar's badge, they were allowed to call out for help as they walked along the roads; but the minute they stopped, they had to shut their mouths – a neat way of keeping them moving through your town or village, methinks!

'EARLY INGRATITUDE'

Take-Away Lunch

Some monasteries and large houses took pity on these poor folk, leaving bread, meat and gravy outside for the gangs of starving strays that used to collect. But later even this was banned and the poor vagabonds were forced to keep away from towns or small communities and could be imprisoned for refusing any kind of work. (Now there's an idea for the unemployed.*)

* You're just so caring and understanding. Ed
Only joking. JF

Chapter 3

MID-KNIGHTS

Knights in the Middle Ages were really just posh soldiers. In return for lands and smart titles from their king, they had to be prepared to don the old tin-wear and fight for him either at home or away. If you were a really smart knight (or a really cowardly one), you could get someone else to go and do your dirty work for you – like a hired gun in a cowboy film – by simply paying the king a fine. This is how we come to hear of these legendary fighters, back from the Crusades, who toured England's green and pleasant lands looking for well-paid war work, freelance dragon-slaying or the odd perky princess who needed rescuing from a castle tower (and a rotten husband).

Useless Fact No. 484

A lot of the knights-slaying-dragons stuff comes from the 'worm' (Old English for dragon) that struck terror into the good folk of Durham in the Middle Ages. Apparently the heir to Lambton Castle caught a small creature like an eel while fishing and promptly threw it down a well. It grew so big that when the young knight was off crusading, it used to come out and eat anyone it came across (there ain't much grub for a growing dragon down wells, you see). Then, full up, it would curl itself round Lambton Hill and go to sleep. When the knight came back, he killed the monster but rather stupidly promised a witch that he'd also slay the first person he met after doing so. Unfortunately, the first along to congratulate him was his dad. Young Lambton backed down on his promise and from then on the Lambton family were cursed. Well, I, for one, believe it.*

*You would. Ed.

Tournaments

Knights would also be expected to 'joust' at tournaments – a sport almost as ridiculous as golf (and almost as dangerous). Two horse-borne knights, in full protective kit, would go to either end of a field and face each other. At a signal from the king, duke, sheriff or someone of equal import, they would charge at each other at full tilt carrying long sticks (lances) – the object of the exercise being to knock the other one off his horse.

Useless Fact No. 486

The playground truce word 'fains' or 'faintes' comes from when knights requested a moment's breather between bouts. It originates from the medieval expression 'Fain I' or 'I decline'.

Tournaments were fairly silly affairs anyway; like pretend wars. When you hear about all those chaps like Robin Hood and Ivanhoe taking forever trying to bash each other with swords and axes, you may not realize that their weapons were purposely blunt, so they couldn't actually do any real harm. I don't know about you, but I think that's a bit of a swizz. You'd never get the Romans or Vikings doing sissy things like that.

OK MATE! KEEP YOUR HAIR ON – I'M ALL YOURS

Once you'd got your opposing knight down, instead of finishing him off, he'd have to call himself and all his possessions well and truly captured and yours (sounds like a playground game).

Then the poor loser would have to ransom himself – that is, buy himself back off the captor (see Very Daft Games in Ancient Times).

Useless Fact No. 489

Now this really is silly. During the Hundred Years' War the English and French would often stop fighting properly so they could have a tournament or pretend battle. War, you see, was regarded almost as a sport, the knights themselves being so well protected that it was only the poor armour-free foot soldiers who got the chop. Anyway, enemies weren't that interested in killing the opposing knights so . . . you've guessed it, they simply captured them and then sold them back to the other side after the battle. Silly or what?

Anyone for Siege?

On the whole, the knights and ordinary soldiers preferred sieges to wars: they were much less dangerous (provided you were the sieger and not the siegee). All you had to do was pitch up outside some walled city or other, threaten them with death and destruction, and then make camp, put the kettle on and sit it out. This could go on for days, weeks, months or sometimes years, with the sieger every now and again sending a few flaming arrows over the wall, or lobbing the odd boulder with one of those catapulty things. Eventually the town would run short of essentials, like loo paper, toothpaste and – oh yes – food, and would have to let the enemy outside in to loot, rape and pillage them (if they hadn't already gone home).

Crusading

If a knight was into making a big name for himself, it was essential to go and fight in far-flung lands. These expeditions were called Crusades or Holy Wars and went on from the en of the eleventh century till the back half of the thirteenth. The main purpose (so they claimed) was to get Jerusalem back from the Muslims, who wouldn't allow Christian pilgrims in, and eventually to conquer Palestine. Pope Urban II urged all the knights and landowners in Europe to stop fighting each other and to become soldiers of Christ. Europe, he told them, was hemmed in by infidels (jolly nasty Muslim people – mostly Turks). If he was to say that now, we'd all probably laugh, but in those days it whipped up everyone big-time, like lighting a huge bonfire smothered in petrol. Everyone hated the Turks and here was a perfect excuse to do something about it.

It was like Red Nose Day in a way. The whole population, from the richest rich to the poorest poor, wanted to get in on the act and soon they were all wearing the red cross symbol of the Crusades on their right shoulder. Indeed, later on, thousands set out for Constantinople, gateway to the East, before the main army. The People's Crusade (as it became known) was simply a ragged bunch of untrained, badly-armed foot soldiers trekking across Europe stealing and begging on their way. Despite this, the Crusades proper started well, and Jerusalem was snatched back in 1099. But hanging on to the place was another matter, and they kept having to go back to sort it – eight times in all.

Useless Fact No. 493

Crusaders in the Middle Ages used a version of the cry 'Hip Hip Hoo___. 'Hip' is supposed to have come from 'HEP', from the ___ their battle slogan *Hierosolyma est perdita* ('Jerusalem ___ hich was a trifle long-winded. 'Hooray' probably comes ___ (Slavonic for 'to paradise') which they yelled as they ___ aughtered their heathen enemies.*

King Dick meets Saladin

Our best Crusader was
Richard I, but he soon came
up against their head man
Saladin – a real tough cookie.
Both men rather admired
each other and even sent
each other little gifts
(ticking ones?).
Unsentimental Richard
mercilessly massacred the
2600 defenders of Acre.
Eventually Acre was
captured back by the Sultan
of Egypt in 1291, which
promptly put an end to a kingdom
founded by the Crusaders.

And the Point of It All?

In the end, the only good to come out of the whole crusading
business was that it pulled the European nations together, and
pushed up the status of the ordinary classes. Why? Because all
the toffs, from knights and barons to royalty, had to sell huge
parts of their estates to the merchants and better-off citizens to
pay for the darn things.

*Mmmm. Not convinced. Ed.

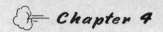

Chapter 4

SERFING IN THE MIDDLE AGES

When William came over and created the feudal system in England, it had already had a trial run in France and most of Western Europe. It seems kinda weird nowadays, but then it was quite common for the poor to put themselves under the protection of the rich (and strong) – literally becoming their property. How d'you fancy that? In return for the land where they could grow grub and build a hovel, a serf and his family would be bound (or bonded) to the Lord of the Manor for life.

How it Worked

It wasn't much different throughout the Christian world: lords and masters owned masses of land split into little parcels, some farmed by freemen but most by serfs, vassals (same thing) or villeins (same thing again . . . again). These parcels followed the open field system and were chopped into strips each of about an acre.

D...... Down

..... /stem was even worse than now; if you were born ...... re was no chance of moving up. You even had to ...... clothes, just so everyone knew how desperately ...... u were. You could get in big trouble if you wore clothes above your station (unlike now, when the very, very rich are often the scruffiest people around!).

Arts and Crafts

Most better-off villages would have a smattering of craftsmen like blacksmiths, millers, bakers and tailors. As villagers usually only had open fires they couldn't bake their own bread or even roast a hen (no turkeys yet) at Christmas, so they relied on the baker. It was the same with their clothes.* Peasant women were not much cop at sewing, so left it to the professionals. Loads of people brewed beer; you only had to put a sign over your front door and hey presto – you'd have an instant pub.

Downsides of Being a Serf

The Lord of the Manor owned nearly everything and nearly everyone. Each serf had a different deal according to the size of his plot. For instance, one might have to pay the boss in kind at various times of the year – a few hens, half a dozen eggs, a bushel of wheat, a good-looking daughter, a strong young son, etc. Also . . .

👑 He'd be expected to work *unpaid* on his boss's land for up to three days a week.

👑 If he used the master's mill, cider-press, oven, animal pens

---

*Why would you want to roast your clothes? Ed.

or tractor (spot the odd one out), he would have to pay for the privilege.

👑 His hovel could be seized at any moment if he upset the Lord or any of his lieutenants.

👑 A young bonded man could only marry a bonded woman and then only one from his parish. This not only created terrible inbreeding but meant he couldn't even improve his lot by hitching up with a rich dame.

On the Other Hand

Serfdom wasn't all bad. It reminds me of our social security benefits system. OK, the chances were that you were never going to get out of the poo financially, but it was probably never going to get much worse either. As long as a family had a lord and master they'd never actually starve to death (get jolly hungry, yes, but never starve). Sometimes the Lord of the Manor would throw huge parties in their honour, with scrumptious feasts and entertaining entertainers. Some serfs even got given gifts – like horses, arms, clothing or even a modest family car*.

* Don't you mean *cart*? Ed

Whoops! JF

So, instead of loathing their master, serfs were often fiercely loyal, and as long as everyone remembered their place and their responsibilities the system worked pretty well. It must also be remembered that there was loads of spare land in medieval England that didn't belong to anyone, on which said serf could feed his animals and chop wood for building, heating and making barbies in the garden.

The Family Hovel

Unlike the ginormous houses of the rich, the average serf's weeny, shed-like house would seldom last more than one generation. They were mostly made of wattle and daub (twigs and clay/mud) on a flimsy wooden frame with a roughly thatched roof.

Size-wise, if peasants did by chance get a bit better off, they simply added rooms on as the family grew. It was common to have the animals living indoors as well as the family. (This wasn't actually much of a problem, as the family were usually just as smelly as the animals.) There would be no chimney but a simple hole in the even simpler roof to let the smoke from the fire in the middle of the room out. You can imagine how foul it was. The only advantage of living in a flimsy house was that it could be easily taken down and moved if so required.

Unserf Me, Sir!

As the Middle Ages wore on, more and more serfs saved up their money and bought themselves back off the boss. Also, during the many uprisings (like the Peasants' Revolt) that were so typical of the middle Middle Ages, some surly serfs would get together and snatch their freedom (and land), to form little free villages.

Useless Fact No. 496

When a serf was officially freed, his master would take him to his front door in front of witnesses and symbolically set him off on the open road (maybe helped along by a highly polished boot?).

That Old Black Death

As you can imagine, the plague caused a severe shortage of labour, thus the ones that survived could call the shots, and even demand their freedom, which was quite a bonus when you come to think of it. Mind you, as many of these ex-serfs became wealthier, they took on their own personal serfs and no doubt pushed 'em around just like they'd been pushed around when serfs themselves. That's progress for you.

A Women's Lot

I hope this doesn't upset my female readers, but those old Middle Ages were no time to be a woman. For a start, the church regarded women as instruments of the devil, both evil and certainly inferior to us men (feel free to debate this point, girls). Because of this the authorities turned a blind eye to severe mistreatment by their hubbies and dads: all wives were regarded as their property to do with as they liked. 'It is plain', said the Canon Law, 'that wives should be subject to their husbands and should almost be servants.' (I'll drink to that.)*
Just to prove the point, the penalty for a mere tiff with your

*I might have guessed. Ed.

BYE DARLING!

husband was a severe soaking (and sometimes drowning by mistake) on the ducking stool in the village duck-pond.

Amongst the upper classes, wives were chosen for how much money or social position was to be gained. The poor rich married ladies were often trapped in their castles, living an almost nun-like existence – sewing, spinning and weaving, playing games on their laptops* or just walking about, while their men were out doing whatever knights did – crusading, jousting, saving dishy damsels and all that sort of stuff.

Mrs Serf

Serfs' wives, poor loves, were regarded as little more than animals and once hitched, it was for life. Marriage took place in a girl's early teens and, having no concept of birth control, it was nothing for them to have had a couple of serflings by the age of fifteen or sixteen.

*Don't you mean laps? Ed

Chapter 5

WHO OWNED WHAT: THE TOFFS BATTLE IT OUT

Most of the violence in the Middle Ages had nothing to do with the poor and underprivileged stealing from the rich, but the rich arguing with the other rich over what (and who) belonged to who (and what). These days rows like this would be settled in court, but then, because land-owners could easily throw together an army, they tended to forgo such niceties, preferring to raid each other's territories, loot each other's mansions, and pillage each other's poultry. They were simply a bunch of upper-class yobbos.

These domestic 'disagreements' often ended in mini-wars with the two enemies bringing in their other land-owning chums to help them. Unfortunately, the poor were usually the ones that got killed but as that's always been the case, we won't make too much of a fuss*. Anyway, these wars never usually went on for too long cos, loaded as they were, even the richest of the aristocracy couldn't afford to Carry On Fighting for ever.

Rebellions Afoot

These little battles were not much of a problem on a national scale but, if the whole country was feeling a bit iffy, there was a likelihood that the tiff could grow until a major rebellion against the king would become possible – which was exactly how the Wars of the Roses started. That war wasn't so much about how powerful the king was, but more about how powerful all those directly under him were.

As I've already said, just about every duke and earl in the country thought he should be sitting on the throne. This sort of thinking led to big trub as the richer and more powerful the rebels were, the bigger the army they could put together and the more of a threat they'd be to you-know-who. Obviously, the king would then go to all his tame dukes and earls who weren't after his job (that week) and promise them extra land and even posher titles if they fought for him. That (in a nutshell) was how civil wars used to come about. The big money, from where I'm sitting, was on sticking with the king (unless it was blinking obvious he was going to lose).

* Typically caring of you, Mr Farman. Ed
I do my best. JF

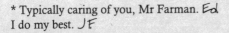

Chapter 6

🗨️ MIDDLE-AGED FOOD

In medieval times, like most times in history, the well-off ate extremely well, and the poor were left scratching around for anything they could lay their hands (or their mouths) on. As you can imagine, it was jolly difficult for your average servile serf to feed his family on the proceeds of a tiny strip of land – let alone give the Lord of the blasted Manor his share. Consequently, getting of food and staying alive became a bit of an obsession. Mind you, if you look at the average overloaded supermarket trolley these days (pushed by the average overloaded supermarket shopper) you might be forgiven for thinking the same thing.

Good Glean Fun

One of the serf kids' main jobs was to go a-gleaning: collecting all the grains that had fallen to the ground during harvest-time, and with crops like peas and beans, collecting any that had been missed at the sides and between the strips of land. They'd also be sent out to gather, scrounge or simply pinch anything that was either growing free, not attached to anything or discarded by somebody richer (a bit like you see in major cities these days).

As you might have guessed, a peasant's diet was not that pleasant. Their bread was heavy and gritty, being either 'maslin', a coarse mixture of wheat and rye, or the even bulkier 'drege' (sounds tasty), a stodgy liaison of barley and oats. They also ate a ghastly kind of porridge made from mushy peas and then washed it down with crude beer. Sounds like my old school dinners (without the beer, unfortunately).

Meat?

In those days, if the peasants wanted meat, they either had to eat each other or, more usually, keep a couple of skinny pigs and a few scrawny chickens,

GOOD NEWS-IT'S YOUR BIRTHDAY. BAD NEWS-YOU'RE THE TREAT!

but these were only to be consumed on special occasions. Most larger livestock (cows, horses, grandparents, etc.) would get a bit nervous as the colder weather approached, as killing and salting them usually meant that they wouldn't have to be fed over the winter.* The menfolk and boyfolk would also snare (no proper guns yet) the odd rabbitfolk and harefolk, and would of course fish (for fish) in the local ponds and rivers. Butter, cheese and eggs were too valuable for the poor devils to eat themselves and would end up at the market to be bought by the next class up.

Useless Fact No. 498

Medieval lords and their wives were always given the best cuts of meat. The servants had to make do with the offal, otherwise known as 'umbles'. Over the years the dish became known as 'umble pie' and later 'humble pie', which is the term used for those who have to show a degree of humility, having been put firmly in their place.

*Wouldn't it *always* mean they wouldn't have to be fed over the winter? Ed

Rich Pickings

The rich, as usual, never went short of anything. For a start, they usually had large herds of sheep and cattle (and serfs), a wonderful vegetable garden, orchards, wineries, breweries – you name it. What they couldn't produce themselves was either supplied by their hardworking smallholders or simply bought from someone else. To give you some idea of the scale of what these fat cats consumed, take a look at what the Earl of Northumberland's household got through in just one year at the end of the Middle Ages:

16,932 bushels (sackfuls) of wheat;
27,594 gallons of ale (1.5 litres each per day);
1,646 gallons of wine;
20,000 pounds of currants;
124 beef cattle;
667 sheep;
14,000 herrings.
This is leaving out all the other stuff:
essentials like venison, larks' tongues,
spaghetti rings and Coco Pops.

Chapter 7

FEELING POORLY
𑁋 IN THE MIDDLE AGES

If you were poor in the Middle Ages (as most people were) getting sick was quite a serious business. You couldn't just ring the doc and get an appointment,* as doctors hadn't really been invented and most medical knowledge (a mixture of old wives' tales and magical mumbo-jumbo) was passed down through generations of womenfolk. Part of the awfulness of the Dark and Middle Ages was the fact that all the dead clever scientific knowledge that had filtered down from the Greeks to the Romans and then gradually throughout the world, had been lost because the church (God bless it) thought science was evil. Illness throughout most of the Middle Ages was regarded as the Devil's Work, you see. The Pope of the time even condemned 219 scientific propositions in 1274 – can you imagine him trying to do that now? Whenever anything like this happens in history, it creates an open house for dodgy ancient customs and far-fetched spells.

— THAT'S MY BOY

*It's not that easy these days, either. Ed

Abroad

That doesn't mean that the situation was the same throughout the rest of the world. The Arabs and the Chinese, to name but a few – er – million, were allowing their science and medicine to chug along nicely, especially the Arabs, who picked up a load of those old Greek manuscripts whilst wheeling and dealing throughout the world.

Tail of Newt, etc.

The medieval approach to curing sickness was distantly related to some of the weirder homeopathic products you see in health food shops these days. If you had a severe pain in the stomach, for instance, you were likely to be made to swallow something like the ground-up root of the stinkwort, the minced spleen of the grass snake, the urine of the toad or the powdered rectum of the leech.* And if that didn't do the trick, it was simply God's way and six foot under for you, without so much as a routine autopsy. Consequently, life expectancy was not much above forty for ordinary folk and if you reached your mid-fifties you were regarded as positively geriatric. Come to that, if you reached your seventies you were a freak – practically museum material!

Useless Fact No. 499

If a child was a little poorly, it was common for mums to go round to the local witch and get a powerful charm to hang round his or her neck, on a single virgin's hair. (There must have been a lot of bald virgins around.)

Monkish Thera-pee

Monks were regarded as having more knowledge than others about all matters medical, even though most of their treatment

* You're making this up? Ed
Just making a point. JF

involved hours of long-winded chanting. One approach was to examine a patient's urine (called Taking the Pi . . . Urine?) and it was not uncommon to see a little line of peasants with samples of their nearest's and dearest's in special little baskets,* queuing outside the local monastery. Luckily, monks were eventually banned from going anywhere near medicine.

HE'S NOT WELL IS HE!

Useless Fact No. 501

Wart-charmers were very popular in the Middle Ages. Their job was to get rid of warts and blemishes with magic spells and stuff. I have it on good authority (*Witch Magazine*) that in rural areas they still use this practice and, even odder, it apparently works.

The Big Three

Top of the pops in the Favourite Medieval Diseases chart were:

- St Anthony's Fire, which was caused by eating rotten bread (Grandmother's Pryde?).
- The good old bubonic and pneumonic plagues (thought to have come from ancient Egypt).
- Leprosy, thought to be caused by eating putrid meat or fish. Lepers were not allowed to mix with anyone else, and

* I don't wish to be picky, but how do you actually keep the liquid in question in little baskets? *Ed* OK – little bottles in little baskets. *JF*

for that reason, leper hospitals (converted houses) were probably the first recognized institutions for the sick. If there weren't any in their area, the poor souls would be shoved out onto the open road and made to ring their bells or clackers (ouch!) to warn others not to come near them (I think that's called preventative medicine). Food might be left out for them, just to stop them coming up to the front door. In many ancient churches you can still find a little enclosed section for lepers well away from the congregation (there's one at Salisbury Cathedral).

One Name for All

Unfortunately many other far less serious diseases were given the same old leprosy label and sometimes people with symptoms as simple as an everyday rash were chucked out in the same way. It must have been Scary-Tyme on the roads of Merrie Olde England: bands of lepers walking one way, thousands of terrified peasants trying to avoid the plague running the other, and as if that wasn't bad enough – columns of spooky hooded 'penitents' who went from place to place whipping themselves, declaring their sins, chanting hymns and wailing incessantly (sounds like karaoke night down at my local), all in the vain hope that it would stop them catching this terrible disease that they reckoned had been sent by God as a lesson for the previous naughtiness-ess-ess.*

Useless Fact No. 503

One type of plague (pneumonic) was much more contagious than the other. It could be caught simply from talking to someone infected (for example, saying 'Go away, you infected person.'). The new victim would usually be dead before tea-time. The English,

---

*Blimey, that was a long sentence! Ed

poor dears, thought at one stage that it would wipe out the whole population, but as I said in Chapter 1, it only managed just over a third.

Useless Fact No. 507
When the plague was at its worst, church bells were rung continually. The noise was thought to dispel the disease. Mmm.

Doctors in the House
By the fifteenth century, most little towns would have had a resident physician of sorts, but although they were supposed to hold a fair share of scientific knowledge, they'd still resort to spells and charms if the more orthodox methods didn't work (and, funnily enough, *they* didn't usually work either).

People were often thought to suffer from having too much blood and, for centuries, the nasty habit of bleeding a patient became all the rage for rich and poor alike. If they didn't want to do it themselves, the physicians would use their pet leeches to suck the blood out for them, albeit in smaller quantities – yuk! It's interesting that the use of leeches to reduce swellings (and, would you believe, maggots to devour infected, cancerous and gangrenous flesh – yum, yum) is becoming popular again now (how jolly), despite all the advances in modern medicine.

I DIDN'T KNOW YOU DRANK HERE

Leech-U-Like

The sort of leech they used was either the *Hirudo medicinalis* (brown speckled leech) or the *Hirudo officinalis* (green leech). Both could be made to disgorge the blood (about an ounce) by sprinkling salt on . . .*

Short Back, Sides and Leg Off, Please.

For centuries, the only person allowed to do major operations (probably because he had the right tools) was the town barber. Actually, if you were to see the state of their haircuts, it might give you some idea of the quality of their surgery. Very often injuries which would be regarded as quite minor these days, would turn out to be fatal (especially after a session at the hairdresser's). Just think, they had no antiseptics, no antibiotics, no anaesthetics** (and no Elastoplast).

Useless Fact No. 509

Tooth-ache was often caused by worms in the root. A good old remedy for it was to take a mutton-fat and holly-seed candle and burn it as near to the tooth as possible without setting fire to the patient. A basin of water was held underneath to catch the hot and somewhat bothered worms as they dived out to avoid the heat.

Quack-Quack

Just like the Wild West, there were hundreds of *triacleurs* (or quacks) – unqualified doctors who sold ridiculous pills, potions and charms to the gullible peasants. Treacle was one of their mainstays. According to them, smothering yourself in that sticky substance cured most things (sounds a bit kinky, if you ask me).

* Excuse me, I hope you don't mind, but could we get off this subject, I'm feeling a little queasy. Ed
** Not true – Girolamo Savonarola, an Italian, was knocking his patients out with little sachets containing henbane, opium and mandrake. Ed
Ah yes, but that was in Italy. JF

Useless Fact No. 511

This treacle business isn't as daft as it sounds. The word comes from the Greek 'theriake', meaning the antidote to an animal bite. Treacle became just a term to describe any ointment that was put on a wound. It later became the name for the sugary syrup because sugar was used ever such a lot in medicine.*

Beg Your Pardon!

Charlatans or not, the poor peasants were totally taken in by these guys and also by the pardoners (or indulgence-sellers): travelling friars who had taken the pope literally in the twelfth century when he allowed monasteries to *sell* documents forgiving people their sins and letting them off the inevitable punishment in hell (see Brilliant Scams in Ancient Times). Even more cheeky were the false-pardoners: guys who dressed up as churchmen and flogged their own cut-price indulgences (see Even *More* Brilliant Scams in Ancient Times).

THIS IS AS SORRY AS I CAN AFFORD

Alchemy

One of the great hindrances to the advance of science, whether medical or otherwise, was the popularity of alchemy, a kind of medieval chemistry and now regarded as quasi-magical hocus pocus. Actually, it sounded quite a laugh – loads of quirky

*You *have* been doing your homework, Mr Farman. Ed

spells, dark scary rooms with bubbling retorts and bits of dead animals in bottles everywhere you looked. The main pursuits of the alchemists were: (1) the search for the Philosophers' Stone: a mythical lump of rock which would unleash the secret of turning ordinary metals into gold; and (2) the quest for the Elixir of Life, a hip drink that allowed the drinker to live for ever. (I bet if they had that on sale at my local, it would go down a storm.)

Alchemy was eventually banned by Pope John XXII (twenty-two to you) in 1316, but few proper alchemists paid any attention. Actually, being able to create gold at the drop of a spell would be a little pointless. After a couple of months of mass-production, it would be no more valuable than any other metal. And as for the Elixir of Life, who really wants to live for ever (apart from me*)?

Useless Fact No. 514

Isaac Newton (falling apples, etc.) is regarded as probably one of the most brilliant minds of all time, but he wasn't that bright in all areas. He apparently went totally bonkers trying to find the secret of the Philosophers' Stone. Likewise, Paracelsus, a famous Renaissance physician, thought he'd cracked the Elixir of Life, but fell to his death down the stairs when drunk (not on the Elixir, I hope) and was never able to tell anyone his formula (tee-hee).

ELIXIR – MY FOOT

MRS PARACELSUS

*And me. Ed

Chapter 8

MIDDLE-AGED CHILDREN

Towards the end of the tenth century, after those dratted Vikings had sloped off to France, Europe decided that it might be time to think about educating its population again. Basically people were divided into three types:

1 Those who told people what to do and who went out and fought wars – *without* being killed.
2 Those who simply prayed – that someone else would fight the wars and do all the hard work.
3 Those who did *all* the blinking work and *did* get killed in the wars.

It follows, therefore, that there seemed little point in teaching kids anything more than they would need in their lives, whichever class they came from.

Aristo-Kids
At the beginning of the Middle Ages it was generally thought more important for the posher children to be tidy and polite than to be able to read. Boys should also be able to hunt, sword-fight and know a bit about the law, magic and geometry. When little, they might be sent to other grand houses to act as pages (a kind of child-swapsies system), or when older, as squires/personal assistants to the main man.

Girls would simply be sent as companions to some other rich person's wife where they would learn spinning, weaving, embroidery and all the other boring stuff involved in running a household.

Middle Kids

Towards the end of the twelfth century, cathedral schools and universities were cropping up all over Europe. Oxford was the first to open in England, copying an idea from Paris. When they felt like a boat race, however, they decided to invent Cambridge – but only for the lads of course (there was absolutely no point in educating girls*). A little later, colleges called grammar schools were set up for those we now call the middle class.

Useless Fact No. 516

Did you know that the term 'dunce' comes from one of the cleverest men that ever lived? John Duns Scotus was a brilliant teacher, but after he died in 1308 all his ideas were trashed and anyone who still believed in them was called a 'Dunser'.

Poor Kids

Serflings, as you might have guessed, were only educated if they were to go into the church. Some were simply handed over to the monks and never seen by their parents again (see Terrible Fates in Medieval Times). There was no shortage of children, however, even though huge numbers died as babies. Having loads of nippers was a positive advantage, as they were esssential to the running of the house or smallholding.

A little boy of seven would be required to herd the geese and sheep on the common, prod the oxen's bums when ploughing and take all the rest of the beasts to water. He wood collect would from the woulds (is that right?) and gather straw and sticks to light it with.

* It sounds like you agree? I hope not. Ed

A girl would help with the cooking, fetch water and collect fruit, herbs and berries from the hedgerows. She would also accompany her mum to market and help her make the cheese, butter and eggs* to sell (hard cash was also essential for the peasant to pay for all the stuff they couldn't produce themselves). When a little older, kids were expected to bring home a wage by working for other villagers or the Lord of the Manor.

* Shouldn't she have helped the chickens make the eggs? Ed

Chapter 9

🌬 *TOWN LIFE*

In the very thick Domesday book that the very bright William the Conqueror ordered to see what he owned, there were over a hundred towns mentioned. All the ones that end in 'burgh' or 'borough' (Scarborough, Middlesborough, etc.) were named by the Vikings while all the 'hams' or 'tons' (Southampton, Durham, etc.) date back to Alfred the Great. Then there were all the towns that grew round harbours, fords and bridges (Portsmouth, Cambridge, Dartford, etc.) and also those that snuggled round castles and cathedrals (Newcastle, Oldchurch, York, etc.).

But the towns in those days were weeny; in 1400 only Norwich, York, Bristol, Coventry and, of course, London had more than a thousand houses. What made a town a town (and not a village) was the wall surrounding it. This would have heavy gates that were closed and guarded during the time between sundown and sunrise ('night' to you) to keep whatever brand of barbarian that might be lurking outside . . . outside.

Why Towns?
I know this might seem a little obvious, but towns grew up to accommodate all the people who didn't want to live in the country.* They would supply all the stuff that the manor-, castle- and palace-folk couldn't make themselves, and acted as a centre for trading with other towns (and, if by the sea, other

*That's astounding. Ed

countries). So if you wanted a clock, iron tools, glass, gold or silverware, a harness for the horse (or the wife), smarter clothes for all the family or whatever, it was into the town for you and no need for Park and Ride.

Doing Your Homework

All the craftsmen lived in identical little houses, similar to those in the country, only not nearly so stinky. Instead of pongy pigs in the parlour or foul fowls in the front room, they had workshops to work in. Most of the trades would stick together, not so much because they were chums, but so that everyone could keep an eye on the competition. So, you'd have all the clock-makers in Clock Street, seamstresses and tailors in Cloth Street, and in Shoe Street you'd have all the shoemakers (a load of old cobblers). As hardly anyone could read, the craftsmen would put up signs with pictures of what they were selling.

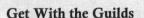

Get With the Guilds

Each craftsman had to be a member of a guild that acted very much like the unions of today (well, like the unions of yesterday). Each member would pay a small subscription, so that if he ever felt poorly they'd look after him, or, if he ever died, they'd look after his family and say prayers for his soul at the funeral. (Fat lot of good that would do.)

Useless and Rather Boring Fact No. 519
If a lad wanted to get into a profession (sorry, girls), he had to serve an apprenticeship for five years. His boss would give him board and lodging, for which his parents would have to shell out.

Streetlife
The narrow streets in medieval towns were pretty disgusting. Mostly cobbled, they'd have an open drain running down the middle, in which *everything* was thrown (yes, even that), providing an *al fresco* (that's outside for 'Italian'*) restaurant for all those disease-carrying rats. The streets would be packed with men, women, children, and all their accompanying livestock (and all their accompanying excrement).

Towns to Rent
Just about all towns were built on land that belonged to some toff or other, who'd be happy to take hard cash for letting people build or trade on their land. As the Crusades became more and more of a drain on the old pocket, the local Lord found himself asking the local townspeople for money . . . The cleverer townies saw a great opportunity and clubbed together to buy their town's freedom. Most medieval monarchs were also well happy to flog the odd town or two to the inhabitants because they were nearly always short of the old readies. When a town achieved freedom it received a Charter which spelt out all the conditions by wh . . . Is this getting boring? I agree. Let's move on.

*Do you mean Italian for 'outside'? Ed

Chapter 10

WITCH REPORT

Everybody loves the idea of witches; old crones in fashionable black, whizzing across the night sky on broomsticks, on their way to or from turning some poor unfortunate into a toad – or worse – a parking warden. Our witch obsession spread throughout Europe in the mid-thirteenth century and ended about a hundred years after what was regarded as the end of Middle Ages. Because this is my book, and because witches were such weird and wonderful people, I'm going to take you right to the end – despite the date.

First of all, what is and was a witch? My dictionary reads as follows:

> NOUN. *Woman practising sorcery;*
> *a fascinating or bewitching woman;*
> *an ugly old hag;*
> *a flatfish resembling a lemon sole.*

As I'd probably find it hard to hold your interest with lemon sole stories for very long, I think I'll go for a mixture of the 'woman practising sorcery' and the 'ugly old hag' scenario.*

*Just get on with it. Ed

Which Witch?

From the time when people first started to live together, they nearly always had someone to whom everyone would go, to give them get-well-soon potions, to frighten away evil spirits, to predict the future, or in some cases, to supply them with hallucinogenic drugs (magic mushrooms, for instance). Far from being hounded to their deaths on a regular basis, these people were regarded as useful members of the community.

Today, the nearest thing to your common or garden witch would probably be the African witch-doctor, though I sometimes worry about some of the wacky things that homeopaths, herbalists and spiritualists get up to, even in these enlightened days.

Useless Fact No. 521

Whenever a church bell was stolen in the Middle Ages, local witches were accused because they were supposed to be afraid of them. A bell dropped into a river by seven witches at Canewdon in Essex has been heard ringing from the deep during fierce storms ever since. I wonder if the river was next to the local pub?

Although witchcraft had been around since Ancient Egypt and Babylon, it was only when those early Christians started throwing their weight around that actual persecution got under way in earnest. They believed that Satan had teamed up with, and was giving a hand to, all those old and out-of-work pagan gods, who needed representatives on earth to carry out their wicked ways . . .

Devils' Disciples

By the thirteenth century, there seemed to be a bit of a surfeit of witches, and someone must have noticed that most of them were little old ladies. Most of the early objections were from religious and church leaders (usually Roman Catholic) who became terrified of anyone who had anything to do with magic, convincing themselves that they must be sucking up to the devil. They also convinced the simple Middle Agers that these women really could fly through the air on broomsticks and that they held wild parties on mountain tops and wind-blown heaths celebrating the Black Mass (sounds quite cool to me).

Going to the Devil

The very first proper witch trial was in 1275 in Toulouse, France. A wrinkly old dear called Angèle de Barthe was up before the beak charged with having improper relations with a demon, and subsequently giving birth to a monster (crikey, even my mother reckoned she'd done that!). Poor Angèle didn't exactly own up to this, but it's amazing how a bit of *le torture français* loosened her tongue.

The first trial that had *nothing* to do with devils, demons, double-glazing salesmen or other associated foul fellows was in 1390 and this time the venue was Paris. It appears a young lady named Jehanne de Brigue saved the life of a guy when on the verge of death (him, that is). He (rather ungratefully) claimed she'd used witchcraft and she (rather sensibly) denied it. Time for a touch of the old torture again. Jehanne gave in but blamed the man's wife for putting a spell on him in the first place. (Women, eh!*) In the end both women were burned, which seems a little unfair – even to me.

Innocent? I Don't Think So

In 1484 Pope Innocent VIII delivered a bull (ouch!**) ordering the severe punishment of witches. All future trial proceedings were then laid down in the infamous and very first bestseller, *Malleus Maleficarum* (Hammer of Witches) by two dodgy Dominican Inquisitors (witch-hunters). The book was a smash hit cos for the first time (printed books were only seven years old) your general public could read about deviant rudery and dirty devils, all wrapped up in a high moral message (a bit like the *News of the World*). It was translated into many languages and as a result over 300,000 old ladies were burned, hanged or drowned throughout Europe. In one German village, the ambitious witch-hunter, Franz Buirmann, managed to hoodwink the authorities into burning half of its 300-strong population, including little kids of three upwards. Creeeepy!

The First Witch-Hunt

In England we had our own top witch-hunter, a chap called Matthew Hopkins, who'd been a small-time lawyer in Manningtree, Essex. He eventually became a big-time 'witch-

*Don't be sexist, Mr Farman. Ed
**What's a bull? Ed In this case, it's a religious law. JF.

finder general' owing to his supposed uncanny ability to root them out. It all started when he became convinced that his own village was a hive of witches. One poor old dear was stripped to the buff and searched for the devil's marks. She was found to have signs of an extra nipple (quite a common evolutionary throwback, I'm told) which was just what the executioner ordered. Hopkins had her tortured and tortured until she confessed to suckling her 'familiars' (popular witch-speak for assistants): a spaniel, a greyhound, a polecat and a rabbit. In the end he managed to arrest thirty-two women, hang nineteen and gave a severe ticking-off to a whole load of pets.

Useless Fact No. 524
A century later, Henry VIII noticed that his own wife, Anne Boleyn, had a similar third nipple and it's rumoured that if he hadn't done her for adultery, he was going have her put on trial for witchcraft.

Nice Little Earner
Matthew Hopkins suddenly became really popular and at six quid a witch (no questions asked) he toured the country chasing even the faintest rumour. He ended up making over a thousand quid in one year (nearly half a million pounds in today's money), and left a trail of old women hanging around the length and breadth of the country.

He perfected a method of finding out who was a witch, at least to *his* satisfaction. It went something like this.

👑 Take one single woman, preferably old (though some were young), bent, warty and with a black cat and twigular broom.

👑 Strip her of her clothes.

👑 Take a sharp object and prick her all over, searching for 'devil's marks'.

👑 If victim leaps into air when pricked, fine, but if there's a single area where she doesn't, it means that spot has been touched by the devil and she's guilty. (I think I might just have leaped up and down anyway*.)

👑 She's now ready to be dealt with in the appropriate manner (i.e. killed).

Pond Life – or Death

A quicker way was to toss the old dear into the village duck-pond. If she floated, it meant she was being helped by the devil and was thus guilty and dragged away to be hanged (if she hadn't died from pneumonia first). If the poor thing sank, she was innocent – but dead. Hey-ho.

Hopkins, rather hilariously, suffered the same fate when an angry mob, suspecting he was only in the witch business for the money, chucked him into a pond. Boringly, he survived, but died shortly afterwards from tuberculosis. This heralded the end of the witch craze that had swept through Merrie Olde England, and a lot of poor old dears slept easier in their beds.

* That's cheating. Ed

Chapter 11

ART, SCIENCE, GOD AND ALL THAT

Art: No Thank You

At the beginning of the Middle Ages were the Dark Ages, a time when anything to do with art or beauty (*à la* Roman or Greek) was given the big thumbs-down by the all-conquering Christian Church, who were on one of their occasional anything-that-looks-remotely-nice-or-fun-is-wicked trips. This actually made life a lot easier for the artists, because they could forget all that nice, rounded, three-dimensional but difficult stuff that had been learned from the Greeks and return to the flat, angular and easier style like that of the long-gone Egyptians. They even stopped bothering to look at nature for colour, tending to use up whatever they had most of. A good example of this new/old style is the Bayeux Tapestry, an embroidered picture supposed to have been done by William's wife Matilda to keep her out of trouble while he was away conquering. He must have been away for ages, as it eventually

turned out to be 70 metres long (good job she wasn't knitting him a scarf). It showed the French trashing the English (for a change) in 1066, in cartoon-like simplicity.

As for the rest of it, anything that looked enough like everyone else's stuff was *in* – especially if it glorified God.

Giotto Saves the Day

Almost overnight, one man in thirteenth-century Florence, Italy, brought art back to life. His name was Giotto di Bondone and, although still banging out all those golden religious moments, he discovered how to show things in three dimensions, using shadows and the mostly forgotten perspective (making things look smaller as they go away).

This caused a rash of brilliant Italian painters, but like most things it took ages for the revival to hit England and it only managed when the Church began losing its vice-like grip on anything creative or pretty. The new style was mostly a cross between the warm, sensitive Giotto-driven Italian lot and the dead-flat, Egyptiany-looking Byzantine school. It became known as the 'International Style' and carried on till the fourteenth century and the Renaissance ('rebirth'), the term used for probably the greatest period in art, starring Leonardo, Michelangelo and all that lot.

Head in the Sand

Although grammar schools and universities were just popping up in the Middle Ages, it's fair to say that it was a period in which hardly any new thoughts, inventions or discoveries took place. And did they care? Not a bit. Not only was all the scientific knowledge of the Greeks and Egyptians long-forgotten, but the whole subject was deeply distrusted, especially by the Church. Most Middle-Agers simply got on with the spirit-zapping process of living, not even daring to dream that life could ever be better or aesthetically more groovy.

Geoff Chaucer (c. 1340–1400)

If you want to know much, much more about the Middle Ages, you could do far worse than dip into *The Canterbury Tales* by Geoffrey Chaucer. This long poemy/book sort of thing describes a pilgrimage in which loads of really different folk meet to go on a kind of Holiday with God. There are 24 separate tales all wound round the main theme of a journey to Kent, and all told by a different pilgrim. *The Canterbury Tales* is seen as far and away the most important English book written during the whole of the Middle Ages, and some say it is one of the finest books ever written in the English language (next to *Noddy and Big Ears' Big Day Out* of course).

Useless Fact No. 527

In 1374, to say 'thanks for a good read', the Corporation of London gave Geoff a lease for life (free!) on a huge apartment right over the actual city gate of Aldgate, in east London. The king, not to be outdone, then promised him a daily pitcher of wine. At least the old boy could get sloshed with a roof over his head (and a gate underneath).

☁️ TIME'S UP

There, I've done it: five centuries in sixty odd pages (very odd pages). I hope you're proud of me.* Of course, some 'learnèd' historians might not think it the most comprehensive account of the Middle Ages they've ever read, but maybe I should remind them that the price of this one wouldn't even buy the introduction to one of theirs – so there. If by any chance you do want to know more about the period (if such a thing is indeed possible), might I suggest the local library – they're bound to have loads on the subject.

If, on the other hand, you've seen quite enough and are ready to move on, dare I suggest you rush out forthwith (or even fifthwith) to your local bookshop and buy another in the series. But don't run too quickly, I'm still writing the darn things.

*Not the word I'd use. Ed